D0616840

Soccer Blaster

by Margo Sorenson

To Jim, Jane, and Jill who gave me the gift of soccer.
To Eric and Jason, U.S. National Soccer Team for World
Cup 2006.

M. S.

Cover Illustration: Greg Epkes
Inside Illustration: Michael A. Aspengren

13 14 15 16 PP 08 07 06 05

Contents

Background Summary

Soccer is the most popular sport in the world. More people watched the 1994 World Cup than any other sports event in history. Hundreds of thousands of people and kids play soccer in dozens of countries. Millions more are excited fans.

Whole countries almost shut down for the World Cup games. Almost everyone watches his or her country play soccer. Fans go crazy. They parade down city streets. Traffic stops. Soccer is all that matters for that day!

The United States hosted the World Cup in 1994. Millions of Americans found soccer a great game to watch.

1

Blast Away!

Renny glanced at Alonzo's soccer ball under his desk. He frowned.

"Hey, man, gonna play with us after school today?" Alonzo whispered across the row of desks.

"Sí. Of course," Enrique said.

Renny slid down in his desk. They had ignored him again. No wonder. They knew he wasn't any good at soccer. The first—and only—time he played with them after school, he had made a fool of himself. It was hard enough being at a new school. Not being a good soccer player sure didn't make it any easier!

"Pack up your books, class," Mr. Monroe said.

Renny shoved his books into his backpack. He was sure he could play better soccer. It was just that … Renny sighed. All right. He hated to admit it. But his life would be a lot different if his dad was around.

The bell rang. He got up with the rest of the kids, but he hung back. Everyone got into little groups. But he was too new. There was no group for him. All the guys seemed to want to do was play soccer. That left him out. He watched Alonzo and his friends as they walked ahead of him.

"You better watch yourself today," Alonzo elbowed Rydell.

"Nah! *You* better watch it," Rydell said. He grinned.

"Who's keeper today?" Howard asked.

"I'm the *man* in goal today," Markus said. He puffed out his chest.

They laughed and hooted at each other all the way down the street.

Renny crossed to the other side of the street. Things could be different. He could be one of the guys, if only he were a better soccer player. And Renny knew his game would be a lot better if his dad were working with him. Like old times.

But wishing for old times didn't make them happen. Why couldn't his dad be home instead of at the treatment center? Renny frowned. He didn't like to think about it. But it was true.

Renny stopped at the traffic light. Across the street, he saw the boys swarm onto the soccer field.

Thoughts of the past crept into Renny's mind. First, his mom ran off to Florida with some guy she met at the restaurant. Then his dad began hitting the bottle pretty hard. Some days, Renny came home from school, and his dad would be passed out on the couch.

The light flashed green. Renny crossed the street. He could hear the guys yelling in their game.

"Mark up! Mark up!"

"Arriba!"

"Shot! Shot!"

Renny sighed. Then Grandma had come and moved in for a while. She got his dad to go to the alcohol treatment center. That's when she and Renny moved back here to her house. New school, new kids. And he had no friends, no dad, no soccer.

Renny stopped in front of the video arcade. It was dark inside. The sounds of beeps and sirens and whistles filled the air. Blinking yellow and red lights flashed. Shadowy shapes huddled in front of the games. Voices swirled out of the darkness at him.

"Aw, *man!*" someone complained.

"Yeah! Gotcha!"

"Three thousand sixteen points!"

What the heck, he thought. He hardly had any homework. He fumbled in his pocket. Yes! Some quarters and a dollar bill. He could play for a little while. Grandma wouldn't mind.

Renny walked in. He looked around. He'd play one of his favorite games.

Wait. What was that in the corner? He hadn't noticed that game before.

"SOCCER BLASTER" read the sign in large, flashing red and green lights. It must be a new game. Funny, Renny thought. No one was playing it. Usually with a new game, lines of kids would be waiting to play.

Renny walked closer. It was huge. He'd never seen so many flashing lights. The joysticks gleamed gold in the glare.

Huh, he snorted to himself. Soccer Blaster, right. He'd probably do *great* at this game. He put down his backpack.

Renny studied the game. It looked pretty easy. On the huge, lighted screen, the soccer players ran down the field. The other team's players tried to take the ball away. Sometimes, they would slide-tackle their opponents. There were injuries too. Sure, why not? he asked himself. He might even learn something.

He dropped two quarters in the slot. Suddenly, a wailing siren pierced his ears.

"SOCCER BLASTER! SOCCER BLASTER! SOC-CER BLASTER!" a voice boomed from inside the game. A crowd roared. On the screen, the players arranged themselves. Renny's heart beat a little more quickly. Two black-and-white shirted referees blew whistles.

Tweeeet!

The blue team began dribbling the ball. Renny gripped the joystick. Slide, push, pull. His hand forced the joystick in all directions. His player still had the ball. He raced down the field. Renny slipped him past two red defenders. He grinned. This was easy.

Then, from out of nowhere, a red player zoomed in next to him. The black-and-white ball twirled away across the screen. The red player dribbled it toward his goal.

"Dang!" Renny said aloud. He grabbed the joystick. He sent his defensive player racing toward the red player. He punched the silver button on the board.

Wham! The red player went down! Renny's blue man had the ball again.

"Yes!" he said, grinning.

Renny's blue player dribbled the ball closer—closer—closer!

"Shot!" Renny said. He punched the gold button.

"Yeah!" he exclaimed. The ball twirled into the goal. The keeper missed it.

"Goal! Goal! Gooooal!" the voice called.

Suddenly, all the lights on the game were flashing. Renny blinked. They were blinding him. Whistles and cheers deafened his ears. He shut his eyes against the glare.

Then, everything was quiet. No—not quite. He heard some voices. His face felt hot—as if he had been running. He opened his eyes.

The arcade was gone! He was standing on the sidelines of a strange soccer field. Where in the world was he?

Lights were still flashing. He blinked. It was photographers. They were snapping pictures of some men practicing soccer on the field.

One of the men stopped running. He looked kind of familiar. Why?

"Hey, Renny," he called from the middle of the field. "Bring me my water, will you?"

What was going on? Where was he? What had happened?

2

Where's the Coach?

Renny's jaw dropped. How did this guy know his name? And why did he look familiar?

"Hey, Renny," the young man called again from the field. "My water! *This* year, okay?" He grinned. He pointed over at the grass near Renny.

Renny looked down. Next to him was a water jug. It was red, white, and blue. There were words on the side of it. Slowly, Renny picked it up. He read, "U.S. National Soccer Team: World Cup."

Renny's heart raced. He stared at the men practicing on the field. No way! What was going on? First he was playing a video game. Then, the next thing he knew, he was standing here watching the U.S. team practice for the World Cup!

The guy jogged up to Renny. "Thanks. Hey, are you feeling okay?" he asked. "You look kind of pale."

"Uh, yeah," Renny mumbled. Sure—if being in a strange time-and-place warp was okay.

The guy took the jug. He tipped his head back. He drank a long time. Sweat dripped down his face.

"Hey, Hoyt! Get back to practice, you bum," someone called from the field.

"Yeah, yeah, yeah," Hoyt said. "Keep your shorts on!" Water sprayed out as he talked.

"Thanks," he said to Renny. He grinned and handed back the jug.

Renny stared at the jug. The World Cup team! He couldn't believe it! But—now that he watched the players, he was sure he recognized some of them from the newspaper. Some had even been on TV.

Renny watched them play. He had been reading about the World Cup in the paper every day. Over 150 countries' teams had entered the tournament. Now only twenty-four were left. The U.S. was playing three games in this round.

The U.S. had to get enough points to get to the next round of sixteen. They had to win or tie. Or at least get more points than the other three countries in their group.

He remembered that the U.S. had played Poland two days ago and won. Their second game was Saturday. Was it against Germany? Yes, he was sure it was. Germany was favored to win the whole thing! The U.S. would have to practice and play hard.

The players raced up and down the field. Sounds of grunts and thuds filled the air.

Boom! Someone booted the ball down the field.

Thwack! Someone else headed the ball.

The guys called and yelled to each other.

"Shot! Shot!"

"Mark up, Trevor, mark up!"

"Marc, Andy, get wide! Get wide!"

The keeper was doing a lot of the yelling, Renny noticed. The keeper dove for a shot across the goal mouth. He batted the ball out of the goal with his outstretched hands. Then he landed flat on the grass.

"Good save, Carlos," Hoyt called.

Carlos? Renny thought. That's right, the keeper's name was Carlos.

"All right, let's take a break," Carlos called. He got up and brushed off grass clippings.

Laughing and joking, the men straggled toward the sidelines. They were breathing hard. Their shorts and shirts were grass-stained. Many of them had scrapes and bruises on their legs. They played tough, Renny thought. And this was only practice!

They grabbed water jugs off the grass. Carlos came over to Renny.

"You haven't heard from Pete, have you?" he asked.

What was he supposed to say?

"Uh—no," Renny said. Was that the right answer? What would happen if the players found out he didn't belong here?

Carlos frowned. "I just don't understand it," he said. He walked over to where the men sat on the grass.

"Renny hasn't heard from Pete either," he told them.

"How can we have a decent practice without a coach?" one guy with a blond buzz cut complained.

"Trevor, we've got five days before our next match," Carlos said. "Pete'll show up. We'll have other practices. Just relax," he said.

Trevor tightened his mouth. "But where is he?" he repeated. "We've missed almost a half day of practice with him. This is bad luck."

"This isn't like Pete," Hoyt said. "Something must have happened."

"He probably had an emergency," Carlos said. "Maybe he's talking to FIFA about what's been happening to the team."

The group suddenly got quiet.

FIFA? Oh yeah, Renny remembered. He couldn't think what it stood for. But that was the group in charge of soccer all over the world. Kind of like a United Nations for soccer. They ran the whole World Cup tournament.

But what was happening to the team? Was something wrong?

Renny moved closer to the team. He listened carefully.

"And then someone mysteriously canceled our hotel reservations," one of the men was saying.

"I just don't like it," Hoyt said. His face darkened. "All this stuff keeps happening to us. Someone's after our team. And when we find out, someone's gonna pay." He turned and booted a ball, hard, across the field.

"It could be just a bunch of coincidences," someone else said.

"I don't like it," Trevor said. "I don't like it at all. It gives me the creeps."

What? Renny wanted to shout. What don't you like? But he couldn't. Everyone would wonder why he didn't know. Speaking of not knowing, Renny wondered what he should be doing.

"Hey, Renny!" Hoyt called. "Wanna practice a little? How about some passing?"

Renny froze. How could he practice passing with a member of the U.S. team? He could hardly pass with guys his own age.

His heart thumped. He walked over to Hoyt. Hoyt was juggling a soccer ball on his knee and foot. He expertly flipped the ball to Renny. Renny trapped the ball with his legs. Whew! he thought. The ball dropped to the grass.

Hoyt jogged about twenty feet away. "Okay," he called. "Pass it!"

Renny tried to pass the ball. It spun out crazily. He felt like a fool. This was awful!

Hoyt grinned. "Nah!" he said. He lifted up his foot. He pointed to the inside of his foot. "Right here," he said. "Remember? Tap the ball with the inside of your foot. Be crisp!"

Renny jogged after the ball. He tried it. It worked! A sharp tap did it.

"Turn your body more," Hoyt said. "Then you'll get it where you want it."

Renny copied him.

Tap, tap, tap. They passed the ball back and forth. The ball flashed black-white-black-white through the grass.

Not bad! Renny thought.

"Hey! Here's Pete!" Carlos called.

Renny let the ball roll past him. He turned around. An angry-looking man slammed a car door and started across the parking lot. He carried a huge equipment bag. He jogged toward them. This must be Pete, the coach. Uh-huh. Renny recognized him from photos in the paper.

The players gathered in a group. They all began talking at once.

"Hey, what's up, man?"

"Where've you been, Pete?"

"We gotta work!"

The man held up his hand. He was frowning. "Okay, okay." He looked at everyone. "Is anyone missing?"

"No," Carlos said. "We're all here."

"Dang!" Pete exploded. "I thought so. Listen," he said, "it was another of those dirty tricks." He shook his head. "Someone is pulling some stuff I don't like. If they think it's a joke, they're wrong."

"What happened?" Carlos asked.

"Yeah, what did they do now?" Hoyt asked, his face angry. "I'd like to kick their…"

"I got a message at the hotel," Pete said. "It was an emergency. Someone said that one of my players had been injured in a car accident and that he was at Mercy Hospital."

"Mercy?" said a guy with a black ponytail. "That's way in downtown Los Angeles."

"Exactly, Andy," Pete said. "I drove for an hour and a half to get there. None of you was registered." He frowned. "So I missed half-a-day's practice for some stupid wild-goose chase."

"Who's doing this?" a red-headed guy asked.

"I'm not sure, Eldo," Pete answered.

"Whoever it is wants us to lose," Andy said.

"I'll bet it's the Germans," Hoyt said. He rubbed one fist into his hand.

"Yeah, or the Poles—ticked off that we beat them," Eldo said.

"Don't go jumping to conclusions," Carlos warned.

"It could be someone who isn't into soccer at all," Pete said. "Just some trickster."

Renny listened. What did all this mean? Who was trying to hurt the U.S. team?

3

Sabotage and Dirty Tricks

"Where's my go-fer?" Pete asked. He turned around. He looked at Renny. "Oh! There you are, kid."

Go-fer? Renny asked himself. Oh, yeah. "Go-for" everything. An assistant! That's what he was! Then it hit him. He was an assistant to the coach of the U.S. National Soccer Team!! No way! Alonzo and the other guys at school would *never* believe this!

"Here," Pete said. He handed the soccer bag to Renny. "Fan mail. I picked it up at headquarters yesterday." He grinned at the guys. "Breaking those little girls' hearts, guys?" he joked. "Hand it out, would you please, Renny?" he asked.

Renny panicked. He hardly knew anyone's name! How could he hand out mail? Renny slowly unzipped the bag. He found a bundle of letters with a rubber band around them. He looked at the first one. Whew! "Carlos?" he said. He held the letter out to Carlos.

"Whoa! Hot stuff! Look at those red hearts all over that envelope!" teased Eldo.

"I know how to break their hearts," Carlos said with a grin. He grabbed for the letter.

Renny read the next one. "Andy Theonides," he read. He gave it to Andy. So far, so good.

Uh-oh. Who was this? "Marc Deshotel?" he read, trying to sound casual.

A muscular guy with curly black hair walked up.

"Trevor Cartwright," Renny said. He looked up. Trevor brushed a hand through his blond buzz. Then he reached for the letter.

Renny handed out the rest. He tried to remember all their names and positions from the newspaper.

There was Carlos Almeida, the goalkeeper and captain, of course. Then Hoyt Bragg, who played forward. Hoyt wanted to punch out the Germans. Renny grinned. Trevor Cartwright was a defender, the one who was so worried about Pete being late. Eldo Honor played midfield along with Tom Wyschaft and Paul Ramirez. Marc Deshotel and Andy Theonides were defenders too.

No one else on the team had gotten fan mail. They looked disappointed.

"Too bad, guys," Hoyt joked. "Better look good for the cameras and reporters next time."

"Let's get moving," Pete said. "One-on-one. To the field," he barked.

"Mano-a-mano," joked Carlos. "Hand-to-hand combat!"

The players followed him onto the field. They paired off.

"Here," Pete said. He held a clipboard out to Renny. "Hold this for me, please. Oh, and Renny," he went on, "tell the video guy we're ready." He motioned to a man standing on the other side of the field. He was holding a video camera.

Renny took the clipboard. He began jogging across the field.

The players were doing some drill one-on-one. One man dribbled. The other guy did everything he could to steal the ball away. *Everything!* Renny noticed. Shoving, pushing, knocking each other around. They were even grabbing onto each other's shirts! That was illegal! Renny guessed they had to be prepared for anything.

"Start filming," Renny told the video guy. Then he jogged back to join Pete.

From the sidelines, Renny watched drill after drill. It almost made him tired. At high speed, the players dribbled a crazy pattern around cones. They did two-on-one drills. Then something called "Bombs Away." They headed balls in the air. All the while, their grunts and yells echoed across the field.

"Hey!"

"Unnh!"

"Watch it! Watch it!"

He wished *he* could be out there, part of the team. But, Renny frowned, he couldn't even keep up with the other guys his age.

Pete blew a whistle. "Come on in," he yelled.

Sweating and panting, the players jogged in. They grabbed their water jugs from the grass.

"We'll run some set plays now," Pete said.

"You sure there aren't any spies around?" Eldo joked. He wiped his mouth with the back of his hand.

"Yeah. What about the dude with the camera?" Hoyt asked. He unscrewed the top of his water jug. "He's not our usual guy."

"It's his partner. You all sound paranoid," Pete said. "Knock it off."

"I wonder why?" Hoyt mocked. "We have a right to feel paranoid. Too many weird things are going on. Like when the bus was late two days ago," he reminded Pete.

"That's right," Andy agreed. "We could have been late to the field for our game against Poland." He spit on the field. "Good thing we always plan to be there a couple of hours early."

"I can't figure out who could have called the bus company and told them we changed to a different hotel," Marc said. He dumped some water on his head. It dripped down his face.

"Probably the same person that left the message for Pete today," Paul said.

"It's those Germans," Hoyt said. "I know it. And I'm gonna do something about it too." He flexed his fingers. "Their captain—Horst Schlosser. He's got an attitude."

"Calm down, hot shot," Carlos said. But he smiled.

"I bet it's the Poles. They want us to lose. That way they have a chance to get back in," Eldo said. "That Vitas Androszinski is one sly dude."

"Oh. That reminds me. I didn't tell you guys yet," Trevor said.

They all looked at him.

"I think someone got into my hotel room last night," he said.

A hubbub of voices interrupted him.

"What?"

"How do you know?"

"What did they do?"

"I couldn't really tell. It looked like they just messed up my stuff. You know, pulled junk out of drawers and tried to put it back and all that," Trevor frowned. "I don't know what they wanted."

"Nothing was missing?" Eldo asked.

"There's nothing to steal," Trevor joked. "From a poor soccer player? Right!"

Carlos had a knowing look. "We can't let this stuff get to us," he said. "That's probably just what they want. If we get unfocused, we won't play our best game. If we don't play our best game, we'll lose. And we need to win. We've got to get to the round of sixteen! So," he looked around the group, "let's quit second-guessing. Let's just play soccer."

"Thanks, Carlos," Pete said. "My thoughts exactly." He looked at everyone. "Let's do our Arsenal Special," he said.

The men dropped their water jugs on the field. They began jogging to their places.

"Renny," Carlos said. He motioned to Renny.

Oh dear, Renny thought. He liked it better when he was in the background, unnoticed. He still felt like such an intruder. Don't let me get caught, he hoped. He walked over to where Carlos stood.

"Listen," Carlos said softly. "I need your help."

"Yeah?" Renny asked. "Okay. Sure." Carlos was a good guy. He'd try to help him.

"You notice things. You're a good observer. I've seen that," Carlos said. He looked at Renny seriously. "I want you to pay special attention to everything that happens with the team. People won't pay much attention to you 'cause you're a kid. And that's good. That puts you in a good spot. Maybe you can help us get to the bottom of all this."

"You mean, help you find out who's messing with the team?" Renny asked.

Carlos wanted him to help! Yes! He wanted to yell and jump up and down. But that wouldn't be cool, he reminded himself.

"Yeah. Just stay in the background. And keep your eyes open," Carlos said. "Be careful, though," he warned. "Whoever is doing all this means business. The stakes are pretty high. But we'll get this joker. Just wait!" He grinned at Renny and gave him a high-five.

Carlos jogged back to the goal. Renny watched him go.

Yes! Renny thought. He felt so important. He'd find out who was pulling all the dirty tricks! But Carlos was right. He'd have to be careful. After all, someone was trying to hurt the U.S. team. And they might try to hurt him too.

4
Sign Those Autographs

Renny looked at the players seated around him on the team bus. Everyone else was talking and laughing across the aisles. They were on their way back to the hotel.

Renny was quiet. He felt uncomfortable. What would he do when they got to the hotel? Where was he going to sleep? Did he even have a room?

The bus pulled up in front of the hotel. Everyone got off. Renny followed them inside.

"See ya at dinner," Carlos called.

"Yeah, sure," Renny said slowly. He raised a hand in a sort of wave.

He stood in the huge hotel lobby for a moment. His eyes were wide. He'd never been inside a hotel before. Sure, he'd seen them in movies. But this was different. He was actually here.

But—now what? What was he going to do about a room? He was trapped. His heart sank. They would find out he didn't belong.

"Hey, Renny," Pete said. He walked up to Renny. He had just left his car with the valet outside. He was holding a card out to Renny. "Here's your key."

He looked at Renny's surprised face. He grinned.

"Don't you remember?" he asked. "You asked me to keep it for you. You were afraid you might lose it on the field." Pete shook his head. "The way you notice things and keep track of them, I can't believe you'd lose anything. But here you are."

Renny took the card. It had holes punched in it. This was a key? How did it work? Renny felt very uneasy.

"Uh, thanks," Renny said. He followed Pete to the elevator. He stared at the card in his hand. It had no numbers on it! How was he supposed to find his room? He felt sweat break out on his forehead. He took a breath.

"Ah, Pete," he began.

Pete looked up from his clipboard. "Yeah?"

"What floor are we on?" he asked. He crossed his

fingers. I hope we're on the same floor, he thought. They had to be.

"Eighth!" Pete grinned at him.

"And I'm room…" Renny stopped. Please, oh, please, he begged silently.

"836," Pete finished. He shook his head and grinned. "Is your brain scrambled by all these dirty tricks?" he joked. "Or is it too many hotel rooms in too many different cities?"

Yes! It worked! Renny heaved a sigh of relief.

The elevator doors swooshed open. He and Pete walked down the hall together. Pete stopped at room 832. Renny hesitated in front of Pete's door. "See you at six for supper," said Renny. As he said good-bye, he watched as Pete slid the card key in a slot in the door. Then he slid it back out again. When green lights near the slot blinked, Pete turned the knob and opened the door.

Whew, Renny thought. What a relief. Saved again. Now he could get in his room without embarrassing himself.

Renny stopped in front of 836. He followed Pete's lead and the card key worked. He walked in. His own hotel room! He couldn't believe it.

Wait! What was he going to wear tomorrow? He didn't have a suitcase—he just had on what he had worn to school. School—that seemed like a million years ago.

Slowly, he walked over to the dresser. He opened up a drawer.

He blinked. His clothes! There was the World Cup soccer shirt his dad had bought him. And his other shirts—and shorts and jeans too.

Renny plopped down on the bed. He shook his head. This was incredible.

He stared out the window at the Orange County hills. But—how and when was he going to get back home? Actually, he was having a lot more fun here. There wasn't any Alonzo to rag on him. No guys ignored him. No one here thought he couldn't play soccer. And they were helping him too. Hoyt had worked with him today.

****

The next morning, Renny met the team for breakfast. At the table, he listened as the players talked about plans for the day. The team was going to a shopping mall this morning. Their major sponsor, Ekony shoes, had arranged for them to meet with a lot of reporters there. It would be great publicity for the team and a lot of free advertising for the shoe company.

"Always the buck—the money," Hoyt said through a mouthful of scrambled eggs.

"Don't complain," Carlos said. "They're paying for your uniform and all your new cleats." He grinned. "Not to mention those TV and magazine ads that are making you a nice little bundle."

"Yeah," Trevor said. He poured himself some coffee. "There wouldn't be a World Cup without the sponsors."

31

Renny listened carefully. He knew about Ekony shoes. They were the best, especially for soccer. Renny knew he'd never have a pair. They cost way too much money. He sighed. And these guys each got as many pairs as they wanted.

The team met the bus outside the hotel. The bus' huge engine vibrated its silver sides. On its side hung a sign. "U.S. National Soccer Team: Ekony Shoes, Proud Sponsor," it read.

"At least the bus is here today," Hoyt said. "No mess-ups this time."

"It's showtime," Eldo joked as they got on the bus. "Now, Trevor, you look pretty for all those cameras and the girls," he said. He laughed as he dropped down into a window seat.

"No one will be looking at me," Trevor answered. He sat down behind Eldo. "It's you, Carlos, and Hoyt that the girls are after. They all think they're in teeny-bopper heaven when you three show up."

Renny listened to the conversations around him. Soon the bus pulled up at the mall.

He stared in awe. There were at least a couple hundred people waiting for them in front of the mall. Adults and kids stood two- and three-deep on the sidewalk. Cameras were flashing. A huge green banner reading "EKONY SHOES PRESENTS THE U.S. WORLD CUP TEAM" hung over the mall entrance. Holy cow! This was definitely the big time.

The team climbed off the bus. The crowd was yelling and cheering.

"Go U.S.A.! Go U.S.A.!"

"Yeah, Hoyt!"

"Arriba, Almeida! Arriba!"

"We love you, Eldo!"

People jostled and pushed. Hands thrust out. In them were pieces of paper and even T-shirts to autograph.

Renny hung back. No one wanted *his* autograph anyway. Once they were inside the mall, a large man and a red-headed woman found Carlos and Pete. They smiled and shook hands.

Those must be the sponsor's reps, Renny decided. Carlos and Pete smiled at the cameras again and again. The other players hung back as Carlos and Pete were photographed.

Most of the crowd had formed a huge line that snaked through the mall. Other people were standing in groups watching.

Pop! Pop! Pop! The sound echoed through the mall.

"Down!" Renny yelled. Gunfire! He knew that sound too well. It echoed through his neighborhood sometimes.

People screamed. Some rushed to the exit. Others dropped to the mall floor.

A mall security guard grabbed the microphone in front of the table. "It's safe! Please be calm," he assured the crowd. "No one has a gun. I repeat—no one has a gun. It's only firecrackers."

Slowly, people got up from the ground. Others came back from the exits. The panic died down. Renny got up. He felt his heart pounding. That was too real.

The guard had a kid by the arm. The kid looked scared. He must have been playing with firecrackers, Renny thought.

Gradually, things returned to normal. Now the photographers were taking pictures of other players. Sometimes, the players held up Ekony shoes. Eldo lifted up one foot and pointed to his shoe with his other hand. He laughed for the camera.

Some of the players sat behind the table. They were signing autographs for each person as the line moved forward.

Renny sat down on a planter. He brought his knees up under his chin. He watched in amazement. I can't believe I'm a part of all this, he thought.

"Hey."

Renny turned around. Trevor was smiling at him.

"Too much, huh?" he asked, gesturing at the scene in front of them.

"Yeah," Renny said. "Yeah, it is."

Trevor sighed. "There's a lot of money in this for the sponsors. Too bad the soccer players don't get more of it."

"Don't they?" Renny asked.

"Some of the players have contracts with Ekony. Carlos and Hoyt do. So does Eldo," Trevor said. "So they actually get paid for their advertisements. They make out fine."

"How about you?" Renny asked.

Trevor frowned. "I'm not a star," he said. "I never will be. I just do my job as a defender. There's not much glory in that, I guess."

Renny nodded. He didn't know what to say.

"Besides," Trevor went on, "I'm not going to make soccer my life, either. Not like these guys will. They'll go on to coach and all that. Not me."

Renny looked at him curiously. "What *are* you going to do?" he asked.

"I want to sail around the world someday," Trevor said. He looked away from Renny into the distance. "That's what I want."

"Sounds great," Renny said. Actually, he hated boats. He got seasick the one time his dad took him out for a little fishing trip.

"Yeah," Trevor sighed. "Some day, some way, I'll get the money to buy my dream boat. Then I'll be gone—sailing the seven seas, as they say." He grinned at Renny.

A soccer ball bounced into the planter.

"Ho!" Trevor said, grabbing it. He looked at Renny. "How about some footwork drills to pass the time while these celebrities show off?" he asked.

"Sure!" Renny said. He hoped he could do them!

He got up and watched Trevor juggle the ball with his foot. Up, down, around. Renny almost got dizzy watching.

"You do it," Trevor said. He flipped the ball to Renny.

Renny concentrated, but the ball kept slipping away. Over and over he tried.

Trevor laughed. "Don't worry! You'll get it. You're already doing better."

Renny felt a tap on his shoulder. He turned around. It was the lady rep for Ekony. She was holding out a green box. "Ekony Excellence," it said on the top.

"Here," she said smiling. "Carlos said the coach's assistant should have a pair too."

"Thanks," Renny said. His hands trembled as he took the box. His own pair of Ekony cleats!

This was too good to be true. Everything was going great for him. Now, if only the team could win on Saturday.

Renny's thoughts of the upcoming game changed his happy mood. He frowned. Someone—somewhere—didn't want the U.S. to win. Someone was pulling dirty tricks. The tricks were getting worse too. They might even get dangerous. Renny shuddered, remembering the firecracker sound.

Then Renny thought about what Carlos had asked him to do. He couldn't let down his guard. He owed it to the team to keep his eyes open. There were only four days left before their next game. He hoped he'd be able to help before something terrible happened.

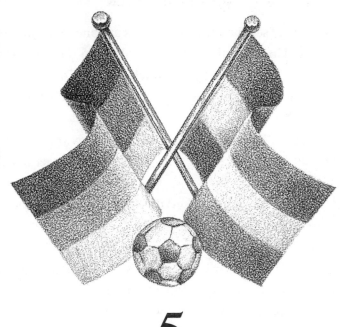

5

The Germans

"Good practice this morning, guys." Pete stood in front of the team in the hotel lobby. "Meet down here in an hour. The bus will take us to the Rose Bowl. Germany plays Bolivia at 2 p.m. It should be a good game. We'll need to pay close attention."

The sweaty players trailed through the lobby to the elevators. Renny followed. He dropped the huge load of practice towels at the desk. He watched the team get in the elevators.

Then he scanned the lobby. Was anyone watching the players? No, everything looked calm. He took the next elevator up. He hadn't been much help to Carlos so far. But, thankfully, nothing else bad had happened to the team.

An hour later, Renny boarded the bus with the team. They set off for Pasadena. Cars going to the soccer match jammed the freeways.

"Everyone wants to see this game," Hoyt called to Renny across the aisle. He grinned. "It'd be nice to see Germany get its you-know-what kicked."

"That won't happen," Carlos said from behind them. "You know Germany's too tough. Bolivia has never scored a goal in World Cup competition."

"True," Hoyt agreed. "Hey, don't you know their captain, Horst Schlosser?"

"Uh-huh," Carlos said. "I played with him one season on the Bayern-Munich team."

Carlos played for a German team? Renny asked himself. Oh yeah. He remembered. That was before there were top pro soccer teams in the U.S. So the best U.S. players actually played in other countries. But when it was World Cup time, they all came back home.

"He definitely has an attitude problem," Hoyt said. "I'd like to adjust it for him." He grinned.

"Do you think it's Germany?" Renny asked them. "Do you think they're the ones pulling all the sabotage?"

"Yeah," Hoyt said. "Definitely. And when we find out

for sure…" He looked at his fists.

"Don't rule out the Poles," Trevor chimed in.

"Poland was pretty angry. They didn't like losing to us," Marc added.

Andy turned around. "It's bad for them if they lose. When they go home to Poland, they're booed everywhere they go. I saw it happen."

"That's because the Poles love soccer. Their team is like a national treasure," Carlos added.

"All right. Everybody out," Pete called.

The players began filing off the bus.

Flashbulbs popped in Renny's face. Everywhere he looked, there were crowds of excited people.

"Look! It's the U.S.!" one girl yelled. "Oh, Carlos, be mine!" She blew him a kiss and giggled.

Hoyt elbowed Carlos in the ribs. "Good goin'!" he laughed.

The team members pushed and shoved their way through the crowds. They found their reserved seats. The stadium was packed. The sun blazed above. Some men already had their shirts off. The smell of sunscreen and popcorn filled the air.

Renny looked around the stands. He could see people waving the red, yellow, and black flag of Germany. Green-, red-, and yellow-striped Bolivian flags fluttered in the breeze. Some people had their faces painted in their country's colors. Others wore shirts colored like their flags. Tension and excitement filled the air.

Renny's heart raced. Here he was, actually watching a World Cup match! He was *with* the U.S. team! Wouldn't Alonzo and the other guys at school love to be in his place right now! He smiled to himself.

Down on the field, the teams were taking warm-up goal shots. They ran at angles toward the goal. Someone fed them a ball from the side. Then, boom! The ball would arc into the goal.

Wouldn't he like to be able to do that, Renny thought. Maybe Hoyt would work with him if he had some time.

Before Renny knew it, the game began. Germany's attacking forwards launched the ball. The crowd rose to its feet. The roars were deafening. It wasn't too long until Horst Schlosser scored the first goal. Then he dropped to his knees, raised his hands, and looked toward the sky.

"What a jerk," Hoyt muttered to Renny.

The fifty minutes of the first half passed in a blur of excitement. Germany led 2-0. The Bolivian defense was no match for the disciplined German attack.

It was half-time. Renny watched the players mill around their benches on the field. He watched the Germans carefully. Were any of them watching the American team?

Renny watched a man in a suit walk up and down behind the German bench. Every now and then he would lean down to talk to one of the players. They wouldn't even turn around to face him, Renny noticed.

"Who's the guy in the suit?" Renny elbowed Carlos

next to him.

Carlos peered down at the field. "Oh, that's Carl Dryden," he said. "He's the U.S. rep for Sparkel Vasser. You know, the mineral water. They're the German team's major sponsor. I met him when I played in Germany." Carlos looked disgusted. "He's weak."

"What's he doing down there?" Renny asked.

"Just keeping a close eye on his money," Carlos said, with a sly grin. "Sparkel Vasser will make a lot of money. That is, if Germany goes to the finals again."

Renny noticed big blue-and-white signs lining the field. "Sparkel Vasser," they read. Behind the German bench were huge blue coolers. Shiny letters on their tops spelled out "Sparkel Vasser." Bottles with blue labels littered the grass in front of the bench. Renny watched as a small boy scurried around, picking them up.

TWEEEEET! The referees' whistles blew. The second half had begun. Renny watched in a daze. The Germans blew through the Bolivians' defenders. Suddenly, one of the Bolivians stole the ball from a German. The crowd roared. One of the Germans got in a slide-tackle from behind. The Bolivian went down, writhing on the grass. The ref thrust a yellow card high into the air. A German player gestured angrily at him. It was Horst Schlosser, the team captain. Horst shook his fist in the air. Then he stalked off.

"Horst got carded!" Carlos said. "Hah!"

"He should get a red card. Then he'd be out of our

game," Hoyt said. "Naah," he added. "I want him *in* our game. I want to show him what for!"

Renny watched Horst slump down on the German bench. What an attitude. Was he the one who was behind all the sabotage?

The final whistle blew, sending the German fans into a frenzy. They stood and cheered and yelled. Cowbells clanged. Horns hooted. Renny thought he would never be able to hear again.

Down on the field, Horst had wrapped himself in a German flag. He began running around the track that separated the soccer field from the stands. The crowd roared as he raced by.

"Let's go on down to the post-match press conference," Pete yelled above the noise. Quickly, the U.S. team got up. They began walking down the steps. The security guards at the entrance to the tunnel waved them on. The tunnel led to the locker rooms.

Reporters already had microphones stuck into the players' faces. Flashbulbs popped. Loud voices echoed against the concrete walls.

Suddenly, Renny felt someone shove him, hard.

"Stupid kid! Dummkopf!"

Renny turned to see who it was. The angry face of Horst Schlosser was about three inches away.

"Americans!" Horst snorted. Then Horst noticed Carlos standing next to Renny.

"So your bus made it on time today, eh?" he sneered.

"Great American organization." Then he pushed his way past them and into the glare of the TV lights. A knot of reporters closed around him.

Renny looked at Carlos. "How did Horst know about the bus?" he asked.

"Good question," Carlos answered. He narrowed his eyes and watched Horst.

The bus ride back to the hotel was quiet. Outside on the city streets, horns honked. People waved German flags from car windows.

Renny let himself into his hotel room. He began washing his face. He was tired.

Bang! Bang! Bang! Someone was knocking on his door. He rushed to open it. Hoyt stood there. His face was red.

"Team meeting in Pete's room, Renny. Now!" he said.

"What's wrong? What happened?" Renny asked. This looked serious.

"All the handles of our extra soccer bags! You know—the ones we leave in Pete's room? All the handles have been cut in half!"

6

Maybe It's the Poles

The team crowded into Pete's suite. Players sat on the floor. They sat on tables. Some leaned against the walls. Everyone was talking at once.

Renny squeezed between Hoyt and Carlos.

"This is giving me the creeps," Trevor was saying in front of him.

"What will happen next?" Marc wondered aloud.

Pete held up his hand. The room was quiet.

"All right. I've alerted hotel security. Obviously, someone found a way to get into this room. So I've had my key changed. All we can do is keep our eyes and ears open." He frowned. "But my main concern is the game Saturday."

"But what about our safety?" Trevor asked. "What if something happens to us?"

"Someone is just trying to shake us up. And your attitude is exactly what the jerk wants," Pete said. "But no one can intimidate the U.S. team. I won't let it happen!"

"We have to stay focused," Carlos said. "We have a chance to get to the round of sixteen. It would be a first for the U.S. Let's not blow it."

"We're going to beat Germany," Pete said. "Just remember that. And watch yourselves, okay? Now, get some sleep. We've got a heavy practice schedule tomorrow."

Talking quietly, the players began leaving.

Hoyt, Renny, and Carlos stood up.

Hoyt's face was dark with anger. "Just wait," he threatened. "Just wait till I get that Horst. Or any of those Germans. They'll be lucky to ever walk again, much less play soccer."

"Cool it," Carlos said. He put a hand on Hoyt's shoulder.

"I mean it," Hoyt said. "I know how to do it. You think you've seen injuries in a game before? Huh! Wait till Saturday."

"We don't need you red-carded," Carlos said. "Don't do anything stupid. Think of the team. Think of winning. That'll be the best revenge."

"I don't play soccer to make friends," Hoyt said shortly. He shrugged off Carlos' hand and walked down the hall.

Carlos sighed. He leaned against the wall and folded his arms. "It's great being captain," he joked.

"Do you think it's the Germans?" Renny asked.

"I don't know," Carlos admitted. "But it's beginning to look more and more like the Germans are responsible. Especially after what Horst said to us. That was pretty stupid of him. Still, we can't rule out the Poles."

"Why would Poland want to do it?" Renny asked. "To get back at the U.S.?"

"Maybe. But they might be hoping to shake us up. If we're too shook up, we might play badly on Saturday. Our total points might end up lower than theirs. Then Poland might have a chance to stay in the competition."

"I get it," Renny said. "But why Poland? Why not some other country?"

"It means the most to Poland. And all of us have had trouble with their captain."

"Vitas Androszinski?" Renny asked. "The one who always kisses the goalposts after he scores a goal?"

Carlos sighed. "Yeah. Another hotdog in international soccer."

"Well, Renny, I need some shut-eye." Carlos waved and walked down the hall.

****

The sun was hot the next morning at the practice field. Renny was sweating as he hurried back and forth with towels and water for the players. He held Pete's clipboard, dialed numbers for Pete on his cellular phone, and shagged loose balls. Being coach's assistant was hard work.

The players ran drill after drill. They yelled to each other. They ran set plays until even Renny knew them all. The team did look tough. Renny was sure they had a good chance to beat Germany. That is, *if* they could stay focused on soccer.

"Break!" Pete called.

The players drifted off the field in twos and threes. Carlos took off his headband. He wrung it out onto the grass.

"It's hot out there," he said.

Hoyt unscrewed the top of his water jug. He turned it upside down over his head.

"Aaaah!" he moaned. Water streamed down his face. His wet hair was plastered to his forehead.

"I've never seen you look so good," Eldo joked.

Renny handed Hoyt a towel. He mopped his face.

"Hey, thanks, kid," he said. He grinned at Renny.

Now is my chance, Renny thought. He cleared his throat.

"Uh—Hoyt? I've been meaning to ask you…" Renny stopped. "Do you think—could you help me with goal shots?"

Hoyt's grin widened. "Sure, buddy." He stretched out a leg. His foot hooked a loose soccer ball. It rolled toward him. Hoyt flipped it up onto his foot. He gave it a back-spin. It jumped up onto his knee. He bounced it a couple of times. Then he let the ball drop to the grass.

"Let's bring you up to speed, kid," Hoyt said. "Go for it," he yelled, booting the ball onto the field.

Renny dropped the rest of the towels on the grass. He raced for the ball. Hoyt jogged behind him. Renny began dribbling the ball toward the goal. He swung his leg back. He aimed for the ball.

Thoomp! Embarrassing! Renny felt his face turn red. The ball squirted out harmlessly to the left.

He heard Hoyt's cleats pound the grass behind him.

"Nah. That's not gonna do it," Hoyt said. He stuck his leg out. "Look at my foot. Lock your ankle." He retrieved a stray ball a few feet away. "Come at the ball at an angle. Like this," he said.

Boom! The ball shot up, up, and then arced into the goal. It would have been an impossible shot for a keeper to stop.

"Wow," Renny said.

Shot after shot, Renny locked his ankle. Breathing hard, he booted the balls. Sometimes, Hoyt would pass to him. Renny would dribble down in front of the goal.

Then he'd take a shot.

Sometimes, Hoyt would cross the ball to him in the air. Then Renny would concentrate on the floating ball. He'd focus carefully. Then he'd boot it toward the goal.

Renny was panting as he dropped to the grass. Hoyt jogged up, grinning.

"Tough work, eh?" he said.

"Yeah," Renny gasped.

"You've already improved," Hoyt encouraged. "Just watch the ball. You'll get it."

The rest of practice passed quickly. Back at the hotel, after showers, the team met for dinner in the special room the hotel had set up for them.

"Yeah," Eldo joked. "The hotel management just wants to keep us rowdies away from the rest of the hotel guests!"

"They don't want your hair to scare them," Andy said. Eldo's red hair always looked like he had just plugged his fingers into a wall socket.

A TV and VCR were set up at one end of the room. During their meals, the team watched tapes of their practices and of other teams' games.

Tonight, Pete chewed his steak intently. He never even looked at his plate. His eyes were glued to the moving players on the screen.

Pete looked at his watch. "Hey," he said. "There's supposed to be a press conference on right now. It's Poland. Vitas set it up. He wants to pump up the press."

"Make himself look good at home?" Andy asked.

"Poor guy."

"Poor guy, nothing," snorted Hoyt. "Talk about grandstanding. Every official in FIFA hates to ref his games. He'll drop on the field on any excuse. Then he'll roll around, moaning. I've seen more players get yellow- and red-carded over his dramatics than…"

"Maybe it's Poland," Trevor said. "Vitas sounds like the kind of guy who would try anything for attention."

Renny stuffed more garlic bread in his mouth. Maybe it *is* Vitas, he thought. No, probably not. Whoever was sabotaging them was sneaky. And Vitas definitely wasn't the sneaky type.

"…do you explain your antics on the field?" A reporter's voice blared from the TV set. The conversation around the dining tables halted. Players stared at the TV.

Renny looked up. Vitas was sitting in a chair. Three reporters sat around him. He kept running his hand through his long, blond hair. Then he hunched over to answer a question.

"They're not antics," Vitas argued. "I am hurt. Other players know how well I play. They want to hurt me."

"Why, the —" Carlos began.

"Shhh," Pete interrupted.

"Like the U.S. team," Vitas said. He leaned over and looked into the camera. "They injured me. The U.S. should be more careful," he added. "They are already having problems. They don't need more."

Renny and Carlos looked at each other.

7

Slashed!

Renny watched the houses slide past the bus windows. It was only 8 a.m. and already hot outside. The practice field would be boiling today. Good thing the bus was air-conditioned.

This would be the team's last practice before their big match. Tomorrow they would play Germany. Millions of soccer fans would be watching the game on TV. Renny smiled to himself. What if Alonzo and the others saw him down on the field? He'd be helping the U.S. players, as he always did. Alonzo and the guys would eat their hearts out for sure.

Renny turned to look at the players seated around him in the bus. They were among the world's best soccer players. They were great guys too. And now he was their friend. It was amazing, but no one had ever questioned his sudden arrival on the scene. He shook his head. This whole thing was so crazy. Most of the time, he was too busy to think about it.

Renny frowned. He still worried about what trouble lay ahead for the team. Pete had ordered new extra bags from Ekony. They were being shipped by air and would arrive today. But who was responsible? Germany? Poland? Some angry fan?

BANG! A huge popping noise echoed through the bus! Renny jumped.

"Hey! What was that?" Eldo yelled. Commotion filled the air. Players shouted and yelled.

The bus leaned to the left. It swerved over two traffic lanes. The driver struggled to control it.

"Flat tire!" the driver yelled over the PA system.

"Great," Marc said to Renny. "Now we'll be late to practice." He whacked the seat back in front of him with a fist.

Renny held onto the seat back. The bus listed to the left. Slowly, slowly, it came to a stop. They were on the edge of a busy highway.

The driver talked into his mike to someone. Then he turned on the PA system again.

"Sorry about this," he said. "Another bus is on its way."

Grumbling filled the air. The players turned around to talk to each other.

"I'm not sittin' in this bus," groused Hoyt. "I'm gonna wait outside."

"Me too," Marc said. He followed Hoyt outside.

Through the window, Renny watched Hoyt and Marc. They walked around the bus. They bent down to look at the tire.

Suddenly, Hoyt jerked up. His face was red. Marc was frowning as he stood up.

"Hey!" Hoyt yelled. He banged the side of the bus to get the players' attention. "Hey!"

Carlos pulled down the window. "What's up?"

"Someone made *sure* we'd have a flat!" Hoyt hollered. "Someone drove about a dozen nails into the tire!" He socked a fist into his other open hand.

Renny sat still. Someone had done it again. But who?

The bus was in an uproar. Players piled out. They swarmed around the tire.

"Gonna knock their brains loose!"

"...complain to FIFA!"

"Horst is a dead man!"

Renny joined the others. He stared at the tire. Sure enough, about a dozen shiny nails were driven into the thick, knobby tire. Someone really did a job on it.

"We coulda been hurt," Trevor said. "This isn't good. I'm getting nervous about tomorrow's game."

"People have been killed for soccer before, you

know," Paul said slowly.

Renny knew that. Once in a while, some crazy guy would shoot a soccer player because he had lost the all-important game. He shivered. Soccer was a game, not life and death. But it looked like maybe someone was trying to change that for the U.S.

Half an hour dragged by before the second bus arrived. The disgruntled players climbed on. They rode to the practice field in silence. The bus doors whooshed open. The players grabbed their bags and walked onto the grass. They zipped open their bags and began putting on their cleats.

"Great jumping Jehosa...!" Hoyt yelled. He jumped up. He was holding his soccer cleats. "This is it!" he yelled, angrily. "This is the end. I'm gonna kill him! I really am!"

The players all looked at Hoyt's cleats. The leather uppers had been slashed to ribbons.

"No!" This was from Trevor. He jumped up too. In his hand were his cleats. They too were slashed.

Pete's face looked white. But his voice was calm.

"Hoyt, shut up and settle down," he said evenly. "You have extra pairs. You have one with you, don't you?"

Hoyt grunted.

"Put them on. You too, Trevor," Pete commanded. "We're gonna practice like we've never practiced before. We have a game to win. I don't want to hear any more about this. Now, let's hustle."

Everyone began lacing up his cleats.

"Renny," Pete called. Renny jogged over. "We'll need to be sure Hoyt and Trevor have an extra pair of cleats here with them on the practice field," Pete explained. "I'll call a taxi. Get their hotel room keys. Take the taxi back to the hotel and bring back an extra pair of cleats for each of them. All right?" Pete asked.

"Sure," Renny said. Ride in a taxi? All by himself? He tried to look casual.

He walked slowly up to Hoyt. Hoyt was still muttering under his breath.

"Uh, Hoyt?" Renny asked.

"What?" Hoyt barked. He looked up. He saw it was Renny. "Sorry, kid. What is it?"

"Pete wants me to go back to the hotel and get an extra pair of cleats for you. I need your key and your room number."

Hoyt dug around in his soccer bag. "Here," he said. He held out the card key. "843," he said. "Get the ones with the new laces, okay?" he asked.

"Sure," Renny said. He put Hoyt's key in his left pocket. He walked over to Trevor.

"I need your key and your room number," Renny said. "Pete wants me to get you another pair of extra cleats. Just in case."

"Oh! Ah—sure." Trevor unzipped his soccer bag. Renny saw all sorts of gear inside. A key ring jangled in Trevor's hand as he rummaged through the bag.

"Here," Trevor said. He handed Renny the card key. "819. And thanks."

Renny ran to meet the taxi. At the hotel, he opened Trevor's room door. He found the cleats. He took one pair. Then he walked down the hall to Hoyt's room.

He was just looking through Hoyt's gear when the maid knocked. "Come in," Renny said.

"Sorry," the woman said. She pulled in the vacuum cleaner.

That's strange, Renny thought. He frowned. Why wasn't the maid surprised to see a strange person in Hoyt's room? He should probably explain.

"Ah—excuse me," Renny said.

The maid stopped changing the sheets on the bed. "Yes?"

"As you know, this isn't my room," he began. "But I'm the team assistant…"

"Oh, that's okay," she interrupted. "You don't have to explain. The nice young man who was in here yesterday told me that this is like an extra equipment room for the team. He said other players would be in and out all the time. Getting shoes and things, you know."

Renny froze. "What nice young man?" he choked.

"I don't know," the maid said. "He was blond. Nice-looking," she said, turning a little pink.

Blond, Renny thought. Hoyt had black hair.

Horst Schlosser was blond.

And so was Vitas Androszinski.

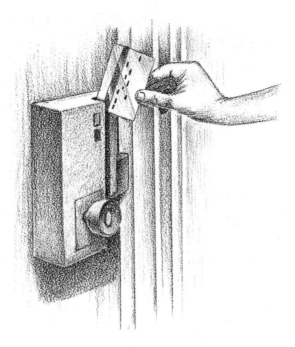

8

Germany Is Dust!

The maid went back to her cleaning. Renny sat still and thought. His heart raced. Okay. How could someone get a key?

He had an idea. He grabbed the pair of cleats with new laces. He raced from the room, down the hall. He jumped into the elevator. Calm down, he told himself. He forced himself to walk slowly.

"Uh—I've got a problem," Renny said to the man at the front desk.

"Yes, sir?" the man asked.

"I—uh—locked myself out of my room. Can I have another key?" he asked.

The man frowned. "I'll have to see identification." he said.

Renny looked downcast. "Oh no. It's locked in my room too. But," he looked at the man, "I can describe what's in the room to you, if you don't believe me. You can come with me and see. Soccer cleats, uniforms…"

The man smiled. "No, no. We don't have to do that. I can tell you're with the team. What's your room number?"

"843," Renny lied.

"Just a moment, please," the man said. He leaned over. He ran a card through a small machine. He handed it to Renny. "There you are," he said.

Renny raced to the taxi waiting outside.

That's how it happened, he told himself. Horst or Vitas had pulled the same trick. It wouldn't be hard to find a player's room number. The hotel was crawling with reporters who would be happy to share the news. And getting a key was no problem. Renny had proven that.

It wouldn't take long to slash leather cleats with a sharp razor. Renny shuddered. It wouldn't take long to slash *anything* with a sharp razor. What would this guy try next?

Renny paid the taxi driver. He raced across the grass with the cleats in his hands. The team was taking a break. They were grouped on the grass. Some of the players rubbed their calves. Others mopped their faces with wet cloths. Some talked quietly about strategy. They used leaves as players and moved them around on the grass.

"Here!" he dropped Hoyt's and Trevor's cleats next to them.

"Thanks," Hoyt said. His mouth was tight.

"Yeah," Trevor said.

Renny spotted Pete sitting a few feet away by himself. Renny hurried over.

"Pete, I gotta tell you something," Renny said urgently. He dropped down next to Pete.

Pete looked at him. "What is it, kid?" He frowned. "Nothing else happened back at the hotel, did it?"

"No—well, kind of," Renny said. "When I was in Hoyt's room, the maid came to clean. She wasn't surprised to see me there. When I tried to explain why I was in someone else's room, she stopped me. She said the guy who was in Hoyt's room yesterday told her that lots of people would be coming in and out."

"The guy who was in there yesterday?" Pete asked.

"Yeah," Renny continued. "She said he was blond."

"I don't like this," Pete said. "I don't like this at all. We need to tell the guys. They deserve to know."

"All right, listen up," Pete barked out to the players.

He told them Renny's story. As Pete explained, some of the players looked worried. Others looked mad. Hoyt looked furious.

Hoyt was the first to speak. "My room? Blond guy? That's Schlosser's tail I'm gonna kick!"

"Hold it," Carlos said. He looked at everyone. "Vitas Androszinski is blond too." He sighed. "And so are lots of other soccer players. And fans too."

"I know it's the Germans!" Hoyt said. He pounded the grass with his fist.

"I'll call FIFA after practice and lodge a complaint," Pete said. "But I won't name the Germans." He looked at the team. "Or the Poles either. I'll just say persons unknown. I just want people to be on alert. And when we find out who is doing this—and we will—it'll be a sorry day for that jerk."

Hoyt shook his head.

"Now, it's back to business. Clear your heads of all this trash. Understand?" Pete glared at the players. "I want your heads in the game. Clear?"

Carlos spoke up. "Pete's right," he said. "We have a soccer game to win."

The players nodded and muttered.

"All right," Pete barked. "Let's play soccer!"

The players got to their feet and jogged back onto the field.

"Hey," Andy said. He walked up to Renny. "It's my turn off. Want to practice some slide-tackling?" He grinned. "It's my specialty!"

Renny knew Andy's nickname, "The Enforcer." He patrolled the backfield as sweeper. He attacked the oncoming forwards. They ended up sprawled on the field.

"Sure!" Renny said.

He and Andy jogged over to the next field.

"Okay," Andy said. "Never slide-tackle from behind." He stopped and smiled. "At least, not when the ref can see you! Just kidding!"

"Dribble away from me," he ordered. He began a slow jog toward Renny.

"Don't use this unless you can't get the ball any other way," he said. "Pick up speed. Then lunge."

Whoomp! Renny landed flat on the field. The ball spun away from him. A few feet away, Andy was sitting on the grass laughing.

"...lunge across the attacker's path," Andy went on, smiling. "Keep your feet first. Stretch out one leg. Slide slightly ahead of the man with the ball. Then you kick the ball away from him with that foot."

Renny grinned. "Okay!" he said. This would be fun. He couldn't wait to learn it. Then he would try it on Alonzo and the others. *If* he ever got back...

Renny scrambled to his feet. He ran at Andy, who was dribbling.

Whoomp! He had missed. He sat on his backside on the grass. Andy stopped dribbling.

"You look surprised!" he said, laughing. He turned

and came back. He gave Renny a hand. "Timing is every-thing in a slide-tackle," he said.

Timing, timing, Renny kept telling himself. Over and over, he missed the tackle. Over and over, he ended up thumping down hard on the grass. But once in a while, he nailed Andy.

"Yeah, little buddy!" Andy hollered. He lay in the grass laughing. "Way to go!"

This *was* the way to go all right, Renny thought. He sat up on the grass, watching the practicing players. Now if they could just beat Germany tomorrow.

9

Renny Has a Hunch

Renny sat bolt-upright in bed. He blinked. The red numbers on the alarm clock read 3:11 a.m.

His heart thudded under his pajamas. It wasn't the Germans! It wasn't the Poles either. He was pretty sure who it was. He just had to find out why. He had to make sure.

Something had been nagging at the back of his mind since yesterday. He had gone over and over the events of the day, trying to figure out what it was. And now he had it.

It was Trevor's key ring. Renny had noticed it when Trevor unzipped his bag to get his room key. Trevor's keys on his ring had jangled. The sound had caught Renny's attention. He had glanced at the key ring.

There was a blue Sparkel Vasser symbol on it. What was Trevor doing with a Sparkel Vasser key chain? Had he ever played for a team sponsored by them? But Sparkel Vasser only sponsored the German national team, didn't they?

So how did Trevor get that key chain? He would have to know one of the Germans. Or Carl Dryden, Sparkel Vasser's rep.

Renny recalled what he knew about Carl Dryden. He was the man who would make Sparkel Vasser lots of money if the Germans went to the finals. And Carlos had said that Dryden was weak.

This was beginning to make sense. Carl Dryden had a pretty strong reason to want another team sabotaged. Lots of money if the Germans kept winning. And, Renny hugged his knees, what would help the Germans get to the finals? Beating a U.S. team along the way, of course. And how could they beat the U.S.? By having the U.S. team shaken up and psyched out by dirty tricks and sabotage. All Dryden had to do was find someone on the U.S.

team to do the dirty work—for money. Trevor had probably been right there for him.

A chill ran down Renny's spine. What else would Trevor try? Injuries? He shook his head.

Renny had to find out about Sparkel Vasser's sponsorship. He would find Carl Dryden tomorrow. He would ask him if they sponsored another team.

Renny's pulse raced. Now he was sure. It was Trevor. The puzzle pieces were falling into place.

He started remembering. Trevor complaining he didn't make enough money. Trevor grousing about not being a star. Trevor saying someone had been in his room, messing it up. Trevor wanting to buy a big sailboat if he could get the money.

Dryden must have set Trevor up. He probably promised him a ton of money to sabotage the team. Then Trevor would fade away, like so many other pro soccer players. He'd sail away with a bundle of loot, never to be heard from again.

And how clever to slash his own shoes. That took the heat off him. It sure made him look innocent.

Renny got up. He opened the drapes to the dark night sky. There were lights sparkling at the base of the mountains. Renny sighed. Trevor was always the one who moaned about being scared. And he had just thought Trevor was a wimp. All along, Trevor was trying to get the team worked up and psyched out.

Man! Renny thought. What some people won't do.

How could someone let his teammates down like that? Just for some bucks. What a jerk!

Renny lay down again. He shut his eyes. The faces of his new friends floated in front of him. Carlos, Marc, Andy, Paul, Hoyt, Eldo, Pete, and all the rest of them. He would really be able to help them now. He could keep his promise to Carlos too.

Morning finally came. Renny was tense during the ride to the stadium. He could barely talk to anyone. Not that the team was talkative before a big match—except Hoyt.

"I'm gonna kick their tails," he kept muttering during the bus ride. His teeth were clenched. He socked the seat in front of him for emphasis.

They arrived at the stadium hours early, as planned. Renny breathed a sigh of relief when the stadium came into view. He didn't know if Trevor had anything planned for the ride.

Renny helped Pete with the equipment. Then he worked with the players to set up their lockers. While he worked, he kept his eye on Trevor. He tried to notice everything that was going on.

Next Renny hustled out to the field. He had to find Carl Dryden.

People were already sitting in their seats, hours before the game. Banners floated in the breeze. Radios blared. Renny scanned the German bench and their side of the field.

There! Talking to an official, was Carl Dryden. Renny took a deep breath and began walking toward him. All he had to do was pretend to be a fan asking questions. He knew Dryden wouldn't recognize him.

"Thank you," Dryden was saying as Renny walked up.

Dryden turned to go.

"Ah—excuse me," Renny stammered.

Dryden turned around. He frowned.

"Yes?" he said impatiently.

He had to play the soccer fan, Renny decided.

"Uh—Uh—are you the German team sponsor? Do you know Horst Schlosser?" Renny asked. He tried to look hopeful.

"Yes," Dryden said. He sighed. "What do you want?"

"Do you think you could get Schlosser's autograph for me?" Renny asked. He almost choked having to ask. Oh well, he told himself. It was for a good cause.

Dryden looked disgusted. "Ask him yourself, kid," he said. He began to turn away.

"Oh, sir?" Renny said quickly. "You don't sponsor any other teams besides the German national team, do you? Like Stuttgart?"

Dryden looked puzzled. "No, kid, we don't. Just the national team. I gotta go." Dryden turned abruptly. He dismissed Renny with a wave of his hand.

"Thanks, sir," Renny said. He turned around and hurried back to the tunnel entrance. Now he was sure it was

Trevor. There were just too many clues pointing to him. Trevor had said too much about wanting money. He didn't feel good about his soccer. He was jealous of the other players. And now the key chain. There was no reason for Trevor to have a Sparkel Vasser key chain. None at all. Unless he had gotten it from Carl Dryden. And Trevor was just stupid enough to keep it too.

Renny had to tell Carlos. Then Carlos could confront Trevor. Trevor would probably cave in and admit it, the wimp. The sooner the better too. Before Trevor pulled something else on the team. Something really dangerous.

10
A Soccer Blaster Finish

"Carlos!" Renny said urgently. He pulled on Carlos' jersey. "I need to talk to you."

"What is it?" Carlos looked puzzled.

"Over here. Please," Renny said. He didn't want anyone to overhear them.

Renny led Carlos out of the locker room. They walked through the tunnel and out into the bright sunshine of the stadium. They squinted after the darkness inside.

"What's up?" Carlos asked. "Why the secrecy?"

Renny took a deep breath. "Listen. I think I know who's been sabotaging the team."

Carlos stiffened. "Who?"

"Trevor," Renny said.

"*What?*" Carlos exclaimed.

Renny explained everything. Carlos listened carefully. Soon he began to nod in agreement. Sometimes, he would shake his head in disgust.

"And so, I think you should tell Trevor we know," Renny finished.

Carlos stared up at the stadium flags. They whipped in the breeze.

"No. Not yet. It *might* not be true, you know. We don't have proof. And I don't want to cause a problem right before the game." He sighed. "It would get the team upset. They wouldn't play focused. And we need all the teamwork we can get for this match."

"But, Carlos!" Renny argued. "What if he does something to the team during the game?"

"We'll take that chance. Security is tight."

Carlos smiled at Renny's worried face. "I'll tell you what. I'll make you a promise. If Trevor dogs one play—if he makes me think for one minute that he's favoring the

Germans by the way he plays today, I'll do it."

"You'll watch him then?" Renny asked.

"You bet. I'll be right behind him in the goal. I'll watch his every move. If he doesn't take out the German forwards, I'll be all over him. You'll see. Deal?" Carlos asked, holding out his hand.

"Deal," Renny said. He shook Carlos' hand.

They jogged back to the locker room. The hours before the game flew by. Renny hurried from job to job for Pete and the players. Get this. Get that. Tie this. Find that. Change this. Fix that.

Finally, the referees' whistles blew. The game began.

Renny sat next to Pete. He drummed his fingers on his knees. He watched his friends playing on the field. The Germans' defense was tough. Soon, it was almost the half. No score.

Then Eldo at midfield zigged and zagged down the field. He ran wide. He crossed the ball to Hoyt. Hoyt eluded the man marking him. He raced toward the ball.

Boom! The ball arced up and over the keeper's outstretched arms!

"Goal! Goal! Goooooaaaal!" The stands erupted in a roar. American fans jumped up and down. They waved flags. Bullhorns boomed.

Grinning, Hoyt ran toward the rest of the team. They slapped hands.

"Yes!" Renny was on his feet. He and Pete grinned at each other.

"First goal," Pete hollered above the din. "Good sign!"

The Germans had the ball. Benno Von Boden streaked down the field. He tapped it off quickly to Horst Schlosser. Renny narrowed his eyes. Where was Trevor? Horst was his man. Horst was wide open. Now Horst sped toward the goal. Trevor should slide-tackle him now!

Renny saw Trevor. He was out of position. Not only that, it looked as if he was limping as he ran slowly toward the action. What a jerk! Renny thought angrily. He jumped to his feet.

"Take him out! Take him out!" he yelled.

The German fans were going crazy.

Just then, Horst swung his foot back.

Boom! A swift, hard kick into the corner of the goal. Carlos dove for the ball. It grazed the tips of his fingers. He missed.

Goal for the Germans! Red, yellow, and black flags waved in the stands. Cowbells clanged. Renny could hardly hear anything above the noise.

Suddenly, Carlos yelled something to the team. Then he sprinted over to the sideline.

"Take Trevor out. Now!" he said to Pete. He gulped for breath.

On the field, the refs were yelling at the U.S. players to hurry up. The crowd was on its feet. Renny watched as the players jogged slowly to their positions. Some of them leaned down to tie their cleats. Carlos must have told them to take their time setting up.

"Delay of game! Call delay of game," a voice called angrily from the stands.

Pete looked surprised. "But..." he said to Carlos.

"Just do it. I'll explain later." Carlos hustled back to the goal.

The refs were still yelling and gesturing angrily at the U.S. players, trying to get them into positions for the game to start again.

Pete sent in Marc. Trevor jogged off, limping.

The refs blew their whistles, the noise shrieking high above the crowd. Renny turned to watch as play on the field began again.

Halftime arrived in a few moments. Carlos raced off the field. He grabbed Trevor by the arm. Trevor looked surprised. Carlos shoved Trevor to the edge of the field. Renny tried to watch. He handed out water and towels to the players, keeping one eye on Trevor and Carlos.

Carlos' face was red. He was shaking his fist and yelling at Trevor.

At first, Trevor yelled back. If only he could hear what they were saying, Renny thought. Then, suddenly, Trevor looked sullen. He looked down at the ground.

Carlos looked disgusted. He spit on the grass. Then he turned and left Trevor standing alone.

Renny watched. Trevor stood still. He stared for a moment at the team. Then he turned and quickly began walking toward the tunnel leading to the locker rooms.

Renny dropped the towels he was holding. He ran up to Carlos.

"What happened?" Renny asked.

"The low-life scum admitted it all." Carlos' eyes still flashed with anger. "He did say that the German players knew nothing about it. It was all Dryden's idea.

"I told him I never wanted to see him again. That he was lucky I didn't want to get a red card for fighting or an assault charge in the middle of a World Cup game." Carlos continued. "And that he was lucky I wasn't Hoyt. Hoyt wouldn't care about an assault charge. Or a red card." Carlos grinned a little.

"So, is he going?" Renny asked. Trevor had vanished into the dark tunnel.

"Uh-huh. I told him he'd better disappear before we got back." Carlos smiled at Renny. "He'll never play pro soccer again. Not when everyone hears about this. And they will. Hey, thanks, buddy. You did it. Who knows what else he had planned?" He gave Renny a high-five.

"Yeah," Renny said happily. "Thanks."

"I'll tell the team. Then we'll play our hearts out for the U.S. of A.!"

Carlos quickly gathered Pete and the team together in front of the bench. He told them what had happened. Pete looked furious. The players' shouts of anger filled the air. Hoyt kicked a ball furiously into the practice net.

"Okay, okay," Carlos said. "That just gives us more

reason to win today. Now focus," he said.

"You know how it's done," Pete added, looking at each player. "Be proud you represent the U.S."

The second half passed in a blur. Passes, crosses, goal shots, slide-tackles, and referees' whistles all jumbled together in Renny's head.

Finally, the last whistle blew. U.S.A. 2, Germany 1!!

"We won! We won!" Renny jumped up and down, yelling.

Photographers swarmed onto the field. Flashbulbs popped. Renny blinked. Where was he?

It was suddenly quiet. The field was gone! In front of him was a video game, lights flashing on and off. It wasn't Soccer Blaster, either. It was called Go For It. He looked around for Soccer Blaster. He couldn't see it anywhere.

Had he imagined everything? Was it all a dream? He shook his head to clear it. He rubbed his eyes and sighed. It was all over.

Renny looked at his watch. It was time to go home. He bent down to pick up his backpack. He froze. There, on top of his backpack, was a pair of Ekony cleats.

Renny grinned. His heart lifted. Yes!

He shouldered his backpack and hurried across and down the street. Alonzo and the others were still playing soccer. Renny took a deep breath. He pressed his face against the chain-link fence.

"Hey!" he called.

Alonzo looked over. He frowned. "What?"

"Can I play?" Renny asked.

Alonzo laughed. "Yeah, sure," he said.

Renny quickly put on his cleats. He jogged onto the field.

In the next instant, he charged Enrique, who had the ball. "Unnh," Enrique grunted.

Renny got the ball! Tap, tap. The ball rolled smoothly in front of him. He dribbled wide toward the goal. He saw Alonzo in front of the goal. He crossed the ball neatly to Alonzo over Rydell's head.

Boom! Alonzo kicked it in! Cheers and shouts went up around the field.

Alonzo came jogging toward him. He was grinning. "Hey, man. When did *you* learn to play soccer like that?"

Renny grinned. "You'd never believe it," he said.